FLY BOY

Andy was about to rap on the window when he saw the door burst open. The two men jumped into the room and grabbed the old man.

It startled Andy, and he jerked his arms, which made him move away from the window. *Wrong way,* he thought. *You're going the wrong way!* He flapped his arms to bring himself back, but in his panic he overreacted. Before he could stop he slammed through the window and onto the floor of the laboratory.

"What the—?" One of the men holding his grandfather turned. "It's a kid. A flying kid!"

Andy stood. "Let go of my grandfather!"

"Your grandfather? Is that right, old man? Is this your grandson? So if we take him and bend him a little you'll tell us what we want to know—is that right?"

"Run, Andy! Get away!" Andrew Hawkes shouted.

OTHER YEARLING BOOKS YOU WILL ENJOY:

JOURNEY, *Patricia MacLachlan*
SHILOH, *Phyllis Reynolds Naylor*
BEETLES, LIGHTLY TOASTED, *Phyllis Reynolds Naylor*
MISSING MAY, *Cynthia Rylant*
AWFULLY SHORT FOR THE FOURTH GRADE,
Elvira Woodruff
THE SUMMER I SHRANK MY GRANDMOTHER,
Elvira Woodruff
HOW TO EAT FRIED WORMS, *Thomas Rockwell*
HOW TO FIGHT A GIRL, *Thomas Rockwell*
HUMBUG MOUNTAIN, *Sid Fleischman*
THE SIXTH-GRADE MUTANTS MEET THE SLIME,
Laura E. Williams

YEARLING BOOKS are designed especially to entertain and enlighten young people. Patricia Reilly Giff, consultant to this series, received her bachelor's degree from Marymount College and a master's degree in history from St. John's University. She holds a Professional Diploma in Reading and a Doctorate of Humane Letters from Hofstra University. She was a teacher and reading consultant for many years, and is the author of numerous books for young readers.

GARY PAULSEN
WORLD OF ADVENTURE

FLIGHT OF THE HAWK

A YEARLING BOOK

Published by
Bantam Doubleday Dell Books for Young Readers
a division of
Bantam Doubleday Dell Publishing Group, Inc.
1540 Broadway
New York, New York 10036

If you purchased this book without a cover you should be aware that this book is stolen property. It was reported as "unsold and destroyed" to the publisher and neither the author nor the publisher has received any payment for this "stripped book."

Copyright © 1998 by Gary Paulsen

All rights reserved. No part of this book may be reproduced or transmitted in any form or by any means, electronic or mechanical, including photocopying, recording, or by any information storage and retrieval system, without the written permission of the Publisher, except where permitted by law.

The trademarks Yearling® and Dell® are registered in the U.S. Patent and Trademark Office and in other countries.

Visit us on the Web!
www.bdd.com

Educators and librarians, visit the
BDD Teacher's Resource Center at
www.bdd.com/teachers

ISBN: 0-440-41228-5

Series design: Barbara Berger

Interior illustration by Michael David Biegel

Printed in the United States of America

May 1998

OPM   10   9   8   7   6   5   4   3   2   1

Dear Readers:

Real adventure is many things—it's danger and daring and sometimes even a struggle for life or death. From competing in the Iditarod dogsled race across Alaska to sailing the Pacific Ocean, I've experienced some of this adventure myself. I try to capture this spirit in my stories, and each time I sit down to write, that challenge is a bit of an adventure in itself.

You're all a part of this adventure as well. Over the years I've had the privilege of talking with many of you in schools, and this book is the result of hearing firsthand what you want to read about most—power-packed adventure and excitement.

You asked for it—so hang on tight while we jump into another thrilling story in my World of Adventure.

Gary Paulsen

FLIGHT OF THE HAWK

CHAPTER 1

The backseat of the limousine was covered in soft brown leather. There was a telephone within easy reach, a television, and a snack bar stocked with sodas, peanuts, and candy. The chauffeur checked the rearview mirror every few seconds to see if his fourteen-year-old passenger needed anything else.

Andrew Carson Hawkes III, or Andy, as his parents had always called him, sat like a statue in the middle of the luxurious seat. Nothing about the car or the trip interested him.

He hadn't said a word since they'd left the airport. His eyelids were half closed and he just sat, emotionless.

His mother and father had been killed while they were out jogging. A hit-and-run driver had swerved onto the sidewalk, taken both their lives, and sped away. It had only been twenty-four hours since the funeral.

Andy was going to live with his grandfather, the first Andrew Carson Hawkes, a frail, eccentric invalid whom he barely knew. Andy had met him for the first time at the service. His grandfather had mysteriously slipped out of the service early. And he had arranged for a neighbor to close up his son's house in California, pack his grandson's belongings, and put him on a flight for Colorado.

Henry, the chauffeur, watched Andy in the mirror for a long moment. The boy was definitely a Hawkes. He had the same dark brooding eyes and strong chin as his grandfather. His hair was a little lighter, but the prominent cheekbones and square shoulders told of his heritage.

Not far from the city of Brookvale, the car rolled to a stop in front of a large black wrought-iron gate with the initial *H* welded into each side. A guard standing in a small brick building waved to them through a plate glass window as the gates swung open.

Henry waved back. Andy stared out the car window at the estate.

The grounds were beautiful and spacious, covering more than two hundred grassy, wooded acres. The car traveled for some time on a newly paved road through a grove of trees and then into a bright green meadow. Now the road was lined with immaculately pruned rosebushes of various colors, which led all the way to the house.

Henry pulled the car into the circular driveway in front of the mansion and turned off the engine. He hopped out and opened the door for his young charge.

Andy stepped slowly from the car, scratching his head and looking up. The mansion was four stories high. Small round terraces jutted out in front of every window and marble figures adorned the facade.

"Whew! I knew my grandfather was rich, but I didn't expect this."

Henry stifled a laugh with a cough. "Yes, well, would you like me to show you to your room, Master Hawkes?"

Andy sighed. "I guess I don't have a lot of choice, do I?"

Henry took a large leather bag out of the trunk and walked toward the front of the house. "Come with me, sir."

They walked up the wide steps and through the solid oak front doors. The inside of the mansion was just as impressive as the outside. The entry floor was marble. An enormous chandelier hung from the ceiling and lush oriental carpets covered the massive stairs leading to the second floor.

"Would you like to use the elevator, sir, or do you prefer the stairs?"

"What? Oh, the stairs are fine." Andy was staring at a row of paintings. They were oil portraits of men and women from past generations. They all had something in common—a small red mark that resembled a pair of tiny wings on the left side of the face near the ear.

Andy's hand went to his own face.

Henry cleared his throat. "Those are your ancestors, sir. I see you've inherited the Hawkes family birthmark. Your grandfather has it too."

"Have you known him long, Henry?"

"Oh, yes. A very long time, sir. I've been in Mr. Hawkes's employ for over fifteen years."

"What's he like? I mean, is he"—Andy twirled his finger around his ear—"you know, loony?"

"Whatever makes you ask such an odd question, sir?"

Andy shrugged. "Never mind. It was just something I heard. I could use a hot shower if you'll show me to that room now."

Henry led the way up to the second floor and opened a door. "Here are your quarters. I hope you'll like them. Mr. Hawkes had it especially decorated for you . . . although neither he nor I was sure what things four-teen-year-olds might appreciate these days."

"It's great." Andy glanced around the room. There was a king-sized bed and a walk-in closet. *You could stick about thirty fourteen-year-old boys in here,* Andy thought.

"The bath is to your left. Would you like me to unpack for you, sir?"

"I can handle it. Thanks."

"Very good, sir. Will you be needing anything else?"

Andy shook his head. "I can't think of anything."

Henry backed out the door, putting his hand on the knob. He paused and cleared his throat. "To answer your previous question, sir . . . no, he's not."

"Not what?"

"Not, as you put it, loony."

Chapter 2

Andy finished buttoning his shirt and sat down on the edge of the bed. The shower had made him feel better. For a while, it had even taken his mind off things—things like losing his parents and having to move away from his best friends to a place he'd never seen before.

He walked to the door and opened it. No one was in the hall. The elevator was just across from his room. He entered it and started to press the first-floor button.

But he hesitated. "I guess if I'm going to be stuck living in this museum, I might as well see what the place looks like." He pushed the third-floor button.

When the doors opened he peeked out. Before him was a long hall almost identical to the one on the second floor.

He stepped back inside and hit the fourth-floor button. The doors opened again to reveal a musty-smelling gray carpet and plenty of dust and cobwebs.

"Hmmm. I'd say the maid doesn't get up here too often," Andy mumbled.

A door at the end of the hall opened and Henry stepped out. He straightened his jacket and took a step toward the elevator. When he saw Andy, he jumped. "Oh my, Master Hawkes. You surprised me. I didn't expect you to be up here."

"I really didn't expect to see you up here either, Henry. What's in there?" Andy pointed at the room.

"In there?" Henry looked over his shoulder nervously. "Oh, supplies, you know. Things like that." He stepped into the elevator. "Shall we go down? Your grandfather is back. He'll probably be wanting to see you."

Andy frowned and studied the door. "Isn't the fourth floor an odd place to store supplies? I mean, it's not exactly handy to the rest of the house."

Henry pushed a button. The doors closed and the elevator started down. "Your grandfather told me to say that he regrets not being here when you arrived. Unfortunately he had a business meeting at the Hawkes corporate offices. Some sort of trouble in one of the laboratories."

Andy forgot about the door for a moment. "What kind of company does my grandfather own?"

"It's compan*ies*, actually. I believe most of them are of a scientific nature. But I'll let your grandfather tell you more about that when he thinks the time is right."

"Why hasn't he ever wanted to meet me before?" Andy asked.

Before the chauffeur could answer, the elevator doors opened on the first floor and Henry stepped out. "If you'll come this way, Master Hawkes. Your grandfather is waiting in the study."

Chapter 3

The only light in the gloomy study was a thin shaft that filtered in through a crack between the heavy velvet draperies. It took a few seconds for Andy's eyes to adjust to the dimness.

"Come in, young man. Let me have a look at you."

The crackly voice came from a dark corner. Andy turned to it. A bent old man with white hair and an equally white mustache sat in a wheelchair, his legs covered with a long rug.

Andy stepped forward. He looked down at the man but didn't say anything.

The old man stared back. Finally he broke the silence. "Well, let's get to it, son. I know you have a lot of questions. We might as well get things out in the open."

"What's the big secret up on the fourth floor?"

His grandfather's eyes opened wide. A chuckle escaped his lips. "Here such a short time and you've already found us out? Don't worry, we'll talk about that later." He studied his grandson's face. "You've got the Hawkes looks—and disposition from the sounds of things. Is there anything else you want to know?"

"Yes, sir. Not that it makes any difference, but why haven't I ever met you before? How come you never came around? Did you have some kind of problem with my dad?"

"No. I loved your father very much." Andy's grandfather cocked his head to one side. "Never take things at face value, son. Always look for what others might miss."

Andy was confused. "I don't understand."

The old man pulled on a cord and Henry appeared at the door. "You rang for me, sir?"

"Yes, Henry, I did. I think we should let Andy in on our little secret. I've been keeping tabs on him through the years. My sources tell me he's a smart boy, trustworthy and capable. And since he's living here now we'd probably have a hard time hiding it from him anyway."

"Whatever you say, sir."

"Good." Andrew Hawkes threw back the rug from his legs, straightened his back, and stepped out of the wheelchair. He was tall and distinguished-looking, and didn't seem half as old as he had before. He winked at his grandson. "See what I mean, boy?"

"Not exactly." Andy frowned. "Why do you pretend to be weak and sick if you're not?"

"A necessary masquerade, my boy. For years a certain criminal element has been after my inventions. They will stop at nothing to get their hands on some of them. What these people haven't figured out is that most of my inventions don't come from my corporations and laboratories. They come from here." He pointed at his head.

Andy looked over his shoulder at Henry. "I thought you told me he wasn't—"

13

"What?" The older Hawkes laughed. "Crazy? That too is part of the charade. I had Henry start the rumor. If the world thinks I'm a little off my rocker, they won't have a clue what's really going on."

"What is really going on?" Andy asked, shaking his head to clear it.

"Are there any servants lingering about, Henry?" Andy's grandfather asked.

"None, sir. The gardener and cleaning service come tomorrow. At present we are alone."

"Very good." Andrew Hawkes rubbed his hands together. "Then let's take Andy up and show him the backbone of Hawkes Laboratories."

CHAPTER 4

"What you are about to see could put you in great danger. You will have to be very careful from now on. If anyone suspects that you know what really lies at the heart of my success . . . well, let's just say they wouldn't think twice about hurting you."

Henry fumbled with a key and then opened the door. He stepped aside so that Andy and his grandfather could go in.

"Wow. This room looks like it's right out of a Frankenstein movie. It must cover the whole fourth floor." Andy watched as a strange blue light danced across an electric wire. He walked past some counters with beakers full of chemicals and stopped at a computer terminal. "Do you know how to work all this? It looks like the cockpit of a jet."

"Not only do I know how, I've instructed Henry. He's been an able assistant, although it is a little hard on him to be the cook, butler, chauffeur, secretary *and* lab assistant. If I had someone I could trust who was interested in learning . . ."

Andy scratched his chin thoughtfully. "I might be interested. But before I decide, tell me what kind of stuff you make up here."

"Why don't you show him, Henry?" Andrew Hawkes sat on a stool and waited.

Henry touched a button and the computer terminal came to life. He punched up a list. "If you want to know more about any of these items, just use the arrow keys."

Andy studied the list. "Is there anything you haven't invented? There's everything from women's makeup to radiation-free cancer treatments in here." He turned in his chair. "But I still don't understand. Why would anyone want to take your inventions away from you?"

"I take pride in the fact that my inventions have always been used for the good of humankind. But once I patent something, it usually makes a lot of money. The people who have tried in the past to steal my ideas are only interested in the money. Kingpins of the underworld have broken into my laboratories. They've made threats on my life . . . and on my son's."

"Wait a minute." Andy sat back in his chair. He sighed heavily. "Are you saying that my parents' deaths weren't accidents?"

Andrew Hawkes's voice was faint. "I don't know. I did everything I could to distance myself from them to ensure their safety. But last week I received a letter. It simply said that I should start watching because someone was going to show me an example of how rough things could get if I refused to hand over my latest invention."

"Did you go to the cops?"

"Not personally. I had Henry take the letter to the police station. Because of my reputation they practically laughed him out of the building."

"But we can't let these people get away with it! There's got to be something we can do."

Andy's grandfather ran his fingers through his hair. "I had the letter analyzed for fingerprints. There weren't any. I also had my lawyer hire a private detective agency. So far they've found nothing."

CHAPTER 5

Andy was up early the next morning. He gobbled down the cereal and fruit Henry had waiting for him in the kitchen and ran to the elevator.

He found his grandfather already hard at work in the laboratory. Andrew Hawkes pointed to a white lab coat and goggles and Andy slipped them on. Then he watched as the older man carefully poured a green liquid with shiny gold flakes in it into a glass test tube. "There. I think I've finally found it. We'll do the other tests later, but I'm pretty sure that's it."

Andy bent down and inspected the tube. The liquid was bubbling and a strange blue smoke rose from the top of the tube. The contents acted as if they had a life of their own. "What is that?"

"That, my dear boy, is what people have been searching for since time began. It is the Fountain of Youth." The old man took a hypodermic syringe and filled it carefully from the test tube. "Shortly I shall use myself as the first subject."

Andy raised one eyebrow. "I don't see a fountain."

"It's a figure of speech, son." Andy's grandfather carefully placed the full hypodermic on a paper towel on the table and turned to Andy. "What I think I have here is an elixir that will fade wrinkles, grow hair, and generally make an old person feel young and energetic."

Andy shrugged. "So it's something for the cosmetic counters in department stores?"

Andrew Hawkes rubbed his temple. "I can see I'm going to have to show you something really amazing if I'm ever going to impress you with my scientific abilities." He moved to a cabinet and pulled out a canvas harness with a small rocket pack attached. "Try this on for size."

"What is it?" Andy put his arms through the openings while his grandfather fastened it in front.

"This is the world's smallest rocket booster. It runs on a tiny plutonium battery. It will never wear out. My company has been trying to convince the army to try it, but so far they've only seen it represented on paper and they think it's impossible. They won't even watch a test of it."

"How does it work?" Andy asked, intrigued.

"Press the button on the shoulder of the harness. Then move your arms, as though they were wings. Try it."

Andy took a deep breath and gingerly touched the black button. There was a tiny explosion inside the rocket and he felt himself being lifted off the ground.

"Hey, this is cool!" he exclaimed, floating a few feet off the ground.

"You better move your arms or you're going to hit the ceiling," Andrew Hawkes warned.

"Right." Andy started flapping his elbows and awkwardly jerked forward. "This is so great. It really works!" He rolled over and did the backstroke. Then he tried a couple of flips.

"Be careful, Andy. Some of the things in the laboratory are irreplaceable."

"How do I get back down?"

"Push the button again. Put your arms out and float to the floor."

Andy landed near a bookshelf. "That was incredible. Can I take it outside later?"

His grandfather smiled. "We'll see. I'm glad I finally found something that interests you. But you have to remember that the things we work on in here must remain secret. And speaking of secrets, I need to show you something." Andy's grandfather moved to the bookshelf. "From now on I'd rather you didn't take the elevator to get here. If the gardener or someone noticed that you were constantly stopping on the fourth floor, they might get suspicious. No one is allowed up here but you, Henry, and me."

"You want me to take the stairs?" Andy unbuckled the harness.

"No." Andrew pulled a thick book titled *War and Peace* from the shelf. The bookshelf turned sideways to expose a passageway.

Andy peered in excitedly. "Where does it go?"

"There are several passages. After lunch you can explore them if you like. And if you're very careful, you can take the rocket booster to the woods and see what it can really do."

"Thanks, Grandfather." Andy put the harness back in the cabinet. "Grandfather?"

Andrew Hawkes was already back at the table, studying the syringe full of green liquid. "Yes?"

"Thanks for letting me stay here and be a part of everything. I guess I kind of understand now why you had to stay away from us before."

His grandfather smiled. "Believe me, having you here is truly my pleasure, Andy."

CHAPTER 6

"Where are you going, Henry?" Andy followed the servant out of the study. "Want to watch me test-drive Grandfather's rocket booster?" He held up his bulky gym bag. "I'm taking it out behind the house to the woods where no one will see me."

"Thank you for inviting me, sir. But I'm afraid I must wait for the cleaning service to arrive. I have some instructions for them about the drapes in the dining room. Last week they were very lax and I may have to fire them if things don't improve."

"Sounds like fun. Oh well, maybe you can come next time."

Andy hurried down the long hall to the back of the mansion. He stepped outside onto an enclosed patio just as a white panel truck with BUSY BEE JANITORIAL printed across the side pulled up in the service driveway.

He decided to wait until the cleaners were gone to try out the booster. He hid the bag behind a potted plant and went down the steps.

He heard voices from behind the truck.

"Now remember what the boss said, Ralph. Try to get the old kook to volunteer the information. The boss don't want no shooting unless we have to. But if it comes to it, we're supposed to make it look like an accident."

Andy froze. He heard the back door of the truck slam shut. He crept around by the front bumper and watched the men carry a vacuum to the front door. He couldn't think what to do, wasn't sure if he'd really heard what he thought he had heard. He shook his head. *Henry. I have to warn Henry.*

The two men stopped on the steps and rang

the bell. Henry came to the door and Andy opened his mouth to yell, but stopped. *If I yell now,* he thought, *they'll just take care of Henry and go ahead with their plan.*

Andy crept to the other side of the truck as the door closed and the men went inside. These men were going to hurt his grandfather. Andy had to somehow get ahead of the men and warn him.

The rocket pack!

He ran to the potted plant, grabbed the gym bag, opened it, and put the pack on. *Hurry,* he thought—*no time to waste.* He buckled the straps and without thinking slapped his hand down on the button.

He shot straight into the air, and before he could stop he was at least a hundred feet over the house. *Down,* he thought, *bring it down.* He pressed the Down button and floated downward until he was even with the fourth floor. He moved to the windows and flew along them until he could see his grandfather inside, writing in a notebook.

Andy was about to rap on the window when he saw the door burst open. The two men jumped into the room and grabbed the old man.

It startled Andy and he jerked his arms, which made him move away from the window. *Wrong way,* he thought. *You're going the wrong way!* He flapped his arms to bring himself back, but in his panic he overreacted. Before he could stop, he slammed through the window and onto the floor of the laboratory.

"What the—?" One of the men holding his grandfather turned. "It's a kid. A flying kid!"

Andy stood. "Let go of my grandfather!"

"Your grandfather? Is that right, old man? Is this your grandson? So if we take him and bend him a little you'll tell us what we want to know—is that right?"

"Run, Andy! Get away!" Andrew Hawkes shouted.

But Andy was already in motion and he hit the man on the right, knocking him away from the table and his grandfather. *One down,* he thought. Then Andy turned to the second man, just in time to catch a fist on the side of his head. It knocked him back, and as he fell the fleshy part of his arm came down on the hypodermic needle still resting on the table. It hit at just the right angle to push the plunger and send the green fluid into his bloodstream.

He jerked his arm back, his hand caught the button on the rocket pack, and he smashed into the ceiling—hard. He tumbled back to the floor, shook his head, stood, and started toward the men and his grandfather.

"Shoot him!" one of the men yelled. "It's the only way to stop him!"

The other man pulled a gun and aimed. Andy saw a bright flash at the same time he felt something slam into the center of his chest.

He tried to stay on his feet. But the room was spinning around him and he started down. He felt light, like a floating bubble, and then everything went black.

Chapter 7

"Master Hawkes, can you hear me? Are you all right?"

Andy groggily opened his eyes. He was in his bedroom and Henry was leaning over him with a worried look on his face.

"What am I doing here? I'm dead . . . or at least I should be. I was shot . . . Grandfather . . . How's Grandfather?"

A stout, balding man with a black bag moved to the side of the bed. "Young man, I can't find anything wrong with you. You weren't shot. You just fainted."

Andy tried to sit up. "I might have fainted

too. But I know I was shot." He looked down at the place on his chest where the bullet had hit him. There was nothing there. Not even a mark. "But how . . . ? I mean, I was hit. I felt it."

The doctor turned to Henry. "The shock of seeing his grandfather killed has traumatized the boy. Better keep him in bed a few days. Here's a prescription for a tranquilizer if he should need it."

"Killed? Is Grandfather dead?"

Henry swallowed. "When the police came they found me gagged and tied up in the pantry. They released me and I immediately took them to the laboratory . . . but it was too late. Mr. Hawkes was gone, and you were lying over him, passed out."

The doctor patted Andy's arm comfortingly. "I wouldn't allow the police to question the boy for at least twenty-four hours. He needs time to get over the shock."

Henry walked the doctor to the door. "Don't worry. I shall take the utmost care of him. His grandfather would have wished it. He is the last of the Hawkeses."

CHAPTER 8

Attending another funeral had been hard. When he returned from the service, Andy went to his bedroom, slammed the door, and pulled off his black tie.

The police had questioned him for almost a full day. He had described the two men and the truck to the best of his ability. Henry had convinced him to leave out the part where he thought he'd been shot.

Andy's mind was numb. Maybe the doctor was right. Maybe he had imagined the whole thing. It had all happened so quickly.

He opened the French doors and walked out onto the terrace. He looked down. From the second story the colorful rosebushes looked like tiny dots. Andy sat on the railing and tried to think.

He remembered coming through the window, then parts of the fight. Then nothing. Wait, something. Yes, the needle. He fell on the needle with the green fluid. Then what? Nothing . . . it was all a fog.

"Think," Andy told himself. Frustrated, he stood up and put his hands on the stucco railing. Without warning, the ancient rail gave way and he felt himself plunging forward into space.

He screamed all the way down until his body smashed in a tangled heap on the concrete below.

Again he felt light; then things went black just as they had that day in the laboratory.

As he came to, he had a curious floating sensation, and then he opened his eyes.

Strange crackling sounds came from his body as the broken bones in his arms and legs painlessly snapped back into place like released rubber bands. He sat up.

"This is impossible. No one could fall from a second-story window onto concrete and then just snap back together." Andy studied his arms and legs. They were fine; not even a bruise or a cut. He stood up. His legs were a little wobbly, but he quickly regained his balance. What was happening to him?

And then he realized—the elixir. That was it! He had accidentally injected it into his system and somehow it allowed him to heal superfast.

"I've got to tell Henry about this." Andy raced into the house and down the hall. The study door was open and he caught a glimpse of the back of Henry's head.

"You'll never believe what just happened," Andy said, running into the room. "I fell from the—" Andy stopped. Henry wasn't alone. A tall blond woman with pretty green eyes was sitting across from him, holding a stack of papers.

Henry stood. "Master Hawkes, there is someone I'd like you to meet. This is Leslie Diamond."

The young woman flashed him a sparkling smile and extended her hand. "Hello, Andy. I've been wanting to meet you."

Andy shook her hand. "Nice to meet you, Ms. Diamond." He turned to Henry. "I've got something urgent I need to talk to you about. Could I see you in the kitchen?"

"But, sir, Ms. Diamond is here on business. She's your—"

"This will only take a minute," Andy interrupted. "It's important."

Henry bowed to the woman. "Will you excuse us please, Ms. Diamond? His grandfather's funeral was today. It has been difficult for him."

"Of course. Take your time."

Andy half dragged Henry to the kitchen. He closed the door and let out his breath. "Okay, here's the deal. You know that stuff my grandfather was working on to make wrinkles and junk disappear?"

Henry nodded. "Of course, sir. He was having some problems with it, as I recall."

"It works, Henry. The Fountain of Youth works! Hit me."

"Excuse me, sir?"

"Go ahead, Henry. Double up your fist and hit me right in the face as hard as you can."

"I could never do that, sir." Henry straightened his jacket. "Now, if that is all, we really should get back to our guest."

Andy sighed. "I guess I'll have to do it myself." He opened a drawer and took out a large knife. "Watch this." Before Henry could stop him, Andy sliced the end of his finger.

Henry grabbed the knife. "Oh, good heavens. What have you done, sir?"

"It'll be okay. I promise." Andy held out his bloody finger. In seconds it healed itself. Not even a faint scar was left.

"It's a miracle!" Henry exclaimed. "How on earth did you do it?"

"It was Grandfather's potion. During the fight I accidentally injected myself with it. Just now I fell from the terrace outside my bedroom, and I don't even have a scratch. Don't you see, Henry? They did shoot me that day, just like I said. Grandfather's mixture saved my life."

Henry lowered himself onto a chair. "He actually did it. If only he could have lived to see it. He would have been so proud."

There was a soft knock on the kitchen door. Leslie Diamond poked her head in. "I hate to disturb you gentlemen, but I just remembered another appointment. Henry, if you'll sign those papers we talked about, everything will be legal. I'll be back to check on Andy in a couple of weeks."

"Check on me?" Andy asked.

Henry stood and straightened his lapels. "Yes, Master Hawkes. I didn't get the chance to explain. Ms. Diamond is a social worker for the state. Since you are a minor with no known relatives, she thought it best that you remain here with me for the time being. When I sign the paperwork, I will become your temporary guardian."

CHAPTER 9

Andy stood looking anxiously over Henry's shoulder. "What do you mean, he made it a practice never to list the whole set of ingredients?"

Henry punched up the Fountain of Youth formula on the computer. "Mr. Hawkes was very worried about his experiments falling into the wrong hands. He would record only a partial listing and leave out one or two elements known only to himself."

"Then how are we ever going to figure out what's in the stuff or what the side effects are?"

"Here's something." Henry enlarged the letters on the screen. "Apparently he'd done a small amount of testing. He's listed a few results."

Andy read them aloud. " 'Gray whiskers turn dark. Older specimens seem to act half their age. Young mice show no signs of aging.' . . . Uh-oh."

"What is it, Master Hawkes?"

Andy sat on a nearby stool. "If my grandfather's data is correct and we can't find any way to counteract the potion, it says that I'm never going to grow up. I'll be fourteen forever."

Henry frowned. "Oh, dear. That would be a problem."

"I'll say. I'll never get to graduate from high school or take my driver's test. And who's going to pay attention to me when I'm supposedly old enough to run Grandfather's companies? I'll still look like a kid."

"Rest assured, Master Hawkes, I'll stay on this problem day and night until I come up with a solution."

"Thanks, Henry. But let's face it. You're not

a scientist, and we can't take a chance on involving anyone else. I'm stuck."

Andy's shoulders slumped as he walked across the room. "I wish Grandfather was here to get me out of this."

"You know, Master Hawkes, there is another way of looking at this."

"Yeah, I'll get to watch all my friends get old and die."

"I was thinking more along the lines of how your grandfather viewed his work. He always invented things for the good of humankind. You could use your unique situation to help people."

"Right. What could I do? Help little old ladies cross the street and not have to worry about getting run over?"

Henry shut down the computer. Then he turned to face Andy. "You are forgetting one thing. You are a Hawkes. I'm sure if you put your mind to it, you'll come up with something. And remember, I'm here to help you."

Chapter 10

Henry tapped on Andy's door. "This package just came for you. Would you like me to bring it in?"

Andy yanked the door open. "You didn't open it, did you?"

Henry's chin went up. "Certainly not."

"Good. Wait downstairs. I have something to show you."

"Is all this secrecy really necessary?"

Andy pushed him out the door. "You told me to think up a way to turn my condition into something useful. Well, I think I have. But you have to wait downstairs to see it."

"Very well." Henry turned and marched down the stairs.

Andy shut his bedroom door and tore open the package. He laid the contents out on his bedspread and reached under his bed for the rocket booster.

Moments later he stood in front of his full-length mirror dressed in brown tights and a feather-covered jacket with long golden wings attached to its back. His face was hidden by a mask of a hawk's face. A wide, flowing cape, with slits cut in it for the wings, hung from his shoulders, and on his feet were shiny brown boots with tiny wings on the sides.

"Not bad." Andy turned so that he could see his back in the mirror. "Now if I can just get Henry to go for it." He moved to the door and yelled, "Henry, are you down there?"

"Yes, Master Hawkes. But there's something you should know."

Andy touched the button on the harness under his costume and the rocket booster fired into action. He leaped over the stair railing and flapped his wings. He made two passes across the large entry and then landed gracefully in the middle of the room.

"Well? What do you think?"

Henry blinked. "I must say, you startled me, sir."

"No, I mean what do you think about my idea?"

"Your idea?"

"You told me to come up with something that would help people. Here it is—the Hawk."

"I'm sorry for being so dimwitted, sir, but I don't quite—"

"Come on, Henry. You've heard of Super Spiderkid and some of those guys, haven't you? Well, you're looking at the latest in a long line of superheroes—the Hawk!"

"I don't know about Henry, but I'm certainly impressed."

Andy spun around. Leslie Diamond was standing in the doorway of the study.

"I'm sorry, sir," Henry said. "I had no idea what you were up to, so I let her in."

Andy fumbled for his words. "That—That's perfectly fine, Henry. I mean, you know, what's wrong with my social worker seeing, uh, one of my birthday presents?"

"Birthday presents? That's funny. Your records say that your birthday isn't until December." Leslie smiled pleasantly.

"It was an early present."

"Listen, Andy, I don't want to pull rank here. But if you and I are going to get along you're going to have to start leveling with me. What's going on?"

Andy looked at Henry. "What do you think?"

"The company has had Ms. Diamond thoroughly investigated, and they report that she is single, dedicated to her work, lives with her cat, and has no contact with gangsters of any kind."

"What!" Leslie stormed. "You have no right—"

"But do you think we can trust her?" Andy asked.

"It appears we have little choice, sir."

Andy sighed. "All right, Ms. Diamond, I'll level with you, but I have to warn you it's a little weird."

CHAPTER 11

"Ms. Diamond's all right, Henry. Except for the part when she tried to wrestle the kitchen knife away from me before I could cut my finger. All in all, I thought she took the whole thing pretty well. Didn't you? You know, for a social worker?"

"Yes, sir, she seems like a very nice person."

"I'm glad she agreed to file the papers letting you be my permanent guardian until I'm legally of age."

"It pleases me that you are happy, sir. Now

about this Hawk business. What exactly does one do if one is to become a successful superhero?"

"Lots of stuff. For one thing, a superhero flies around making the world a safer place to live. And maybe as the Hawk I'll be able to catch the guys who killed my parents and grandfather."

"I see. And you intend to accomplish this by . . . ?"

"Come on, Henry. I'm new at this. We'll just have to handle each case as it comes along."

"Very good, sir. When do we start?"

"How about right now? We could go save someone from being mugged or something."

"And what will my duties be?"

"You'll be close by in the car in case my arms get tired from flapping. But don't worry." Andy handed Henry a small radio transceiver. "We'll talk to each other with these. See—I have one strapped to my wrist. If I need you, I'll call."

The telephone on the kitchen wall rang and Henry answered it.

"Hello? . . . Oh, dear . . . I see . . . No,

I've never heard of him. Mr. Hawkes never mentioned it." Henry sighed. "Very well, I'll bring him right down . . . I suppose. If you say so . . . Good-bye."

"What's wrong, Henry?" Andy asked.

"It's awful, Master Hawkes. That was Ms. Diamond. She says a man was waiting in her office when she returned. He claims to be your uncle Harvey."

"My father never talked about having a brother. The guy probably read about Grandfather in the paper and is trying to horn in on his money."

"I hope you're right, sir. However, Ms. Diamond says he has a legitimate birth certificate naming Mr. Hawkes as his father."

"I'm telling you he's a fake, Henry. What else did she say?"

"A very odd thing. She added that you could bring your suit if you wanted to. There might be a need for it."

Andy's forehead wrinkled into a frown. "She must be talking about the Hawk suit. But why would there be a need for it? Un- less . . ."

"You don't suppose Ms. Diamond is sending us a message of some sort, do you?"

"I'm not sure, Henry. But let's put the suit in the limo just in case. Oh, and one more thing. My grandfather wouldn't happen to have anything we could use for a weapon lying around, would he?"

"Mr. Hawkes did not believe in firearms, sir." Henry's face brightened. "But he did have two prototypes of nonlethal self-defense mechanisms."

"Speak English, Henry."

"I'll do better than that, sir. I'll show them to you."

Andy waited while Henry went upstairs. In a few minutes he was back, carrying two polished wooden cases. He set them on the counter and flipped the lids open.

Inside each box, resting on a red velvet cushion, was a strange-looking silver gun.

Henry took the first one out. It was bulky and had a large square barrel. "This is the Gloop Gun." He pointed it and pulled the trigger. A wad of brownish yellow goo shot out of the end and splattered against the side of the garbage can.

Andy moved closer to examine it.

"Don't touch it, sir. It's an extremely powerful glue that would take quite some time to remove."

"That's incredible, Henry. What does the other gun do?"

Henry put the Gloop Gun back and gingerly picked up the second gun. It was shaped like a banana and had a red trigger. "I have never actually used this one, sir. Mr. Hawkes called it a Super Stun Gun and thought it might be useful to the police. I don't know for certain that it even works."

"Pack them in the car along with the Hawk suit. If Ms. Diamond is in trouble, she won't be for long."

Chapter 12

"Here we are, sir. Ms. Diamond's office is on the second floor. Room 202."

"Park in front, Henry. And remember, if things turn out bad in there, don't worry about me. Take care of yourself and Ms. Diamond."

"Yes, sir. Anything else, Master Hawkes?"

"Yeah. No matter what I say or do, just play it cool."

"Cool, sir?"

"You know—go along with whatever I do."

"Of course, sir." Henry stepped out of the car and went around to open Andy's door.

Andy jumped out onto the sidewalk and tucked the back of his shirt into his jeans. "Let's go expose an impostor, Henry!"

"Whatever you say, sir."

They walked into the lobby and waited for the elevator in silence. When it reached the second floor, Henry led Andy to Ms. Diamond's office.

He opened the door and let Andy go in first. A secretary was talking on the telephone. She held her hand over the mouthpiece. "Can I help you?"

"Yes." Henry stepped forward. "Master Hawkes is here to see Ms. Diamond. I believe he is expected."

"Go right in. It's the third door on the left."

Henry led the way down the hall and tapped lightly on the door.

They heard Ms. Diamond ask them to come in. Andy pushed open the door and found himself staring into the beady eyes of a sharp-faced man with a long nose.

"This is your uncle Harvey, Andy," Leslie said tensely. "He wants to take you out to dinner, or perhaps to the zoo, so he can get to know you better."

"I must say, this is a bit sudden," Henry protested. "We don't even know for certain if this man is Master Hawkes's uncle."

The man's eyes narrowed. "Show them the papers, Ms. Diamond."

She quietly pushed a stack of paperwork across her desk. "By the way, Andy, did you bring your suit?"

Andy nodded. "You mean the blue one you wanted me to have dry-cleaned?"

"Uh, yes, that's the one. You might want to wear it to dinner. Why don't you go down and get it?"

"Okay." Andy started for the door.

"Hold it. Nobody's going anywhere." A door that led to an adjacent office opened, and a big man with rust-colored hair and a wide flat face stepped in, holding a pistol. "Can't you handle anything, Harvey? The kid was about to get away. They're on to you. Tie up the geezer and the woman and we'll take the kid for a ride until he feels like telling us where his grandpa's secret formula is hiding."

Harvey scowled and jerked the lamp cord out of the wall to use as a rope. "I was doing all right, Smoke. You didn't have to bust in like that."

"Yeah, you were real good. In another minute the kid would have been long gone."

"Now, Henry!" Andy yelled.

Henry grabbed Leslie and dove for the floor. Andy pulled the Gloop Gun out of his pocket and fired at Harvey. It plastered one of Harvey's hands to the wall behind him. The man struggled but couldn't free himself.

Smoke raised his pistol but changed his mind and jumped through the adjoining door, slamming it behind him. His footsteps were loud as he ran down the hall.

Andy helped Ms. Diamond to her feet. "Call the police and tell them what's going on."

"All right, but where are you two going?"

"Ms. Diamond," Andy whispered, "the Hawk is on his first big case."

CHAPTER 13

"I've spotted him, Henry," Andy said into his wrist transmitter. "Turn on Seventh Street. He's driving a blue Firebird with white stripes on the sides."

Henry put his head out of the limousine window and looked up at the sky. He could barely see Andy above the rooftops. "Aren't you getting a little too high, sir? You wouldn't want to pass out."

"I'm fine. Besides, what's the worst that could happen? I bust up, I heal. All in a day's work for the Hawk. Concentrate on finding that Firebird."

"I see him now, sir. He's pulling off the street into an old warehouse."

"Be careful, Henry. Don't let him spot you."

"I'm pulling over here, sir. What do we do now?"

"I'm going in to get a better look. You stay out here and keep an eye on things. If I'm not out in fifteen minutes, call the cops."

Andy flew to a wide ventilation grate in the roof of the warehouse. He worked a corner loose and slid inside.

Not wanting to attract attention, Andy stopped flapping his wings and stood on a thin steel beam near the warehouse's ceiling. Below him, several men were busy repainting brand-new cars and changing their license plates. The Firebird was parked in a corner, but Smoke wasn't in it.

Cautiously Andy worked his way across the narrow beam to a wooden catwalk that led to an office. He could hear Smoke inside, talking on the telephone.

"Things didn't go like we planned, Boss.

The kid got away and they got Harvey . . . Yes, sir . . . Yes, sir . . . You want me to come up to the big house? But it wasn't my fault. The kid had a gun . . . Yes, sir." Smoke hung up the phone and kicked the wall. "Stupid high-class bigshot. What would he know about kidnapping, anyway?" He stormed out of the office, yelled something at one of his men, and headed down some stairs to the Firebird.

"Hey, look up there, Smoke. It's a giant . . . bird?" One of the painters had lifted his goggles and was pointing directly at Andy. The rest of the workers stopped what they were doing and stared.

Andy pushed the button on his rocket harness and shot across the warehouse.

Chapter 14

"That was a close one, Henry. They didn't get a good look at me, though. I was too high. They thought I was a giant bird."

"Very good, sir. Can you still see the car?"

"He just turned up Rockwood. Take a right at the next light. Now he's pulling into a private drive with a bunch of oak trees in front."

"This is quite impossible, Master Hawkes. I know this house. It belongs to Clayton Townsend—Mr. Hawkes's lawyer."

"Hmmm. That explains a lot of things. Did

61

Grandfather ask Townsend to do the paper-work for all of his invention patents?"

"Almost always, sir."

"Then that's how he knew about the Fountain of Youth. Park the limo, Henry. I'm going in after him."

"Do be careful, sir. And . . . good luck."

"Thanks." Andy swooped over the trees and landed near the swimming pool. He studied the large Spanish-style house, looking for an entrance where he wouldn't be noticed.

"Are you Big Bird?"

Andy tripped on the end of his wing as he whirled around. A little girl about four years old with curly black hair was staring up at him.

He relaxed. "No, I'm the Hawk, a brand-new superhero."

"Too bad. I was gonna ask you to come to my birthday party."

"Oh. Listen, do you know what's in that room right up there?" Andy pointed to an open window on the top floor.

"Yup. That's my sister's room. She's silly. She likes boys. I gotta go now. My mom is

taking me to buy a new dress for my party."
Without another word, the little girl skipped
across the lawn and around the corner.

Andy pushed the button on his harness and
drifted up to the window. It was a girl's room,
all right. Everything was frilly and there were
posters of rock groups and movie stars on the
walls. He could hear running water coming
from behind a closed door. *Good, she's in the
bathroom,* he thought.

He put one leg through the window and
turned off the booster. The door opened and a
girl about his age stepped into the room wear-
ing a towel. Her eyes widened and she opened
her mouth to scream.

"Don't do that." Andy hopped into the
room on one foot and fell over his right wing.
He rolled and landed on his feet. "I can explain everything."

The girl edged over to the window and
looked down. "How did you get up here?" She
took a cautious step toward him. "It's a little
early for trick-or-treating, don't you think?"

"Yes. I mean no. I'm not dressed for Hallow-
een."

"Really? You could have fooled me. What are you, then? Another goon my stepfather has hired to make sure I don't run off with the silver?"

"You're Clayton Townsend's daughter?"

"Stepdaughter. He's my mother's fifth husband—she keeps trying. Hey, you don't sound like you're very old under there." The girl walked around him. "You were going to explain what you're doing here, remember?"

"Uh, maybe later. Right now I've got some business to take care of. See you." Andy opened the bedroom door and peered out. A curved staircase wound its way to the bottom floor. He punched the button and floated down.

The girl stood on the landing, watching. "That's a neat trick," she called down. "You'll have to show me how you do it sometime. I'm free this weekend, if you want to fly by." She disappeared into her room and shut the door.

Andy could feel himself blush under his mask. He shrugged it off and began searching for Smoke and Townsend.

Angry voices were coming from down the hall.

"You've ruined everything, you two-bit hustler! I knew I should have hired a professional. You're worse than those other two goons I had."

"But, boss, I—"

"Don't talk, just listen. Before Harvey spills everything to the cops, I want him out on bail and the two of you on your way to Mexico along with those other two idiots who botched the robbery at the Hawkes mansion. Do you understand?"

"Yes, sir."

"Sorry, Mr. Townsend. But I'm afraid *I* don't understand." Andy stood in the doorway with his feet apart and his wings outstretched, trying his best to look like a superhero.

"It's the bird from the warehouse!" Smoke said, staring. "What's a bird doing here?"

"I don't care who it is! He's heard everything." Townsend pounded his desk. "Get him, you moron!"

Smoke reached into his jacket.

"I wouldn't do that if I were you." Andy unclipped the Super Stun Gun.

Smoke laughed. "What are you gonna do, Bird Man? Shoot me with your banana?"

Andy pulled the trigger. For a second nothing happened. Then, suddenly, Smoke froze in place. His hand was still in his coat and his eyes were glazed.

Townsend drove his portly body into Andy, knocking him off balance and making the Super Stun Gun fall to the floor. The lawyer grunted and brought his fist up into Andy's chin, pounding out two of his front teeth. Then he grabbed an iron paperweight from the desk and slammed it into Andy's head, knocking him unconscious.

Townsend stood over him, breathing hard. "If you want something done right, you have to do it yourself." He moved to his desk and had picked up the phone when he heard something behind him.

The lawyer turned just in time to see Andy sit up and rub his head. "That one stung a little." He felt in his mouth. Both teeth were back. *It's great,* Andy thought. *Works every time.*

Townsend watched, his mouth open, as Andy unclipped the Gloop Gun. Then he ducked behind his desk. "Don't shoot! I don't know who you are or why you're here, but I'll pay you double whatever you're getting if you come to work for me."

"I'm the Hawk, Mr. Townsend. And I work for . . ." Andy stopped to think. "Oh yeah, for the good of humankind."

Andy fired the Gloop Gun over the top of the desk and a big round yellow blob of Gloop landed in Townsend's hair and somehow also managed to catch his right foot, pinning the side of his head to his shoe, a position his body had never enjoyed before. Townsend grunted and rolled around on the floor, picking up bits of paper when he knocked over a wastebasket.

Andy watched until he heard the high-pitched blare of sirens outside. He glanced at his watch. He'd been in here longer than he'd intended. Henry must have gotten worried and called the police. Andy had just enough

time for a good finish. He moved to where
Townsend had come to rest, stuck to the side
of a chair leg.

"The police are on their way. You'll have
plenty of time to think about this day while
you're rotting in jail. And when you do, don't
forget that it was the Hawk that put you
there."

CHAPTER 15

"Listen to this, Henry." Andy shook out the front page of the newspaper. " 'Millionaire lawyer Clayton Townsend confesses to crimes of fraud, burglary, accessory to attempted kidnapping, and murder. While being questioned by police, Townsend claimed to have been captured by a large, talking bird. He is calling the winged creature "the Hawk." He also claims this same bird glued his head to his foot. Prosecutors discount the story, calling it an attempt by the noted lawyer to credit a possible plea of insanity, although they remain puzzled by the fact that one of Townsend's partners seemed to be frozen for three days.' Hmmm. Maybe the Super Stun Gun is set a little high."

Andy folded the paper. "We're on our way to being famous, Henry. Someday the police will probably call in the Hawk to help them on some of their really tough cases."

"Yes, sir. Sir . . . ?"

"What is it, Henry?"

"Might I ask why you are still dressed in the Hawk suit? I had hoped you might take the weekend off. I had some laundry to do and a bit of shopping."

Andy picked up the Hawk headpiece and slipped it on. "It's like this, Henry. I found out that this superhero stuff has a few added bonuses. And one of them told me she was free this weekend if I wanted to fly by."

"I see. And would you like me to follow along in the car, Master Hawkes?"

Andy smiled and hit the button on his rocket booster harness. "Not this time, Henry. I'm pretty sure I can handle this one by my-self."

GARY PAULSEN
ADVENTURE GUIDE

SUPERHEROES

What is a superhero? You probably think of Superman, Batman, Wonder Woman, or Spider-Man when you hear that word. The word *superhero* means a fictional hero having extraordinary or superhuman powers. But it can also mean an exceptionally skillful or successful person—which means that you too can be a superhero!

Just for fun, design your own superhero. First pick out an animal you really like. It could be a high-flying bird (like the hawk), a quick-moving cat (a jaguar or a tiger), or a mighty and powerful beast (an elephant!). Or, instead of an animal, pick out a quality you think is really cool. For example, Stretch Armstrong could stretch his arms way out like rubber bands to capture bad guys.

Pick a name for your superhero, and then start drawing a picture of what you think he or she might

look like. If you picked out an animal, make sure your superhero has some of the qualities of that animal in his or her costume, just like Batman's batlike ears and cape. Then figure out what kind of special powers your superhero has and how he or she might use them. Your superhero's powers should match the kind of creature he or she is. For example, Spider-Man can spin a net for a trap and climb up the sides of buildings, just like a spider.

Then make up a story for your superhero. And be sure to make up some villains for your superhero to fight. Write the story down, or draw your own comic-book adventure starring your superhero.

If you could be any superhero, which one would you choose to be? Why? Do you know anyone you would consider a superhero?

Don't miss all the exciting action!

**Read the other action-packed books in
Gary Paulsen's
WORLD OF ADVENTURE!**

The Legend of Red Horse Cavern

Will Little Bear Tucker and his friend Sarah Thompson have heard the eerie Apache legend many times. Will's grandfather especially loves to tell them about Red Horse—an Indian brave who betrayed his people, was beheaded, and now haunts the Sacramento Mountain range, searching for his head. To Will and Sarah it's just a story—until they decide to explore a newfound mountain cave, a cave filled with dangerous treasures.

Deep underground, Will and Sarah uncover an old chest stuffed with a million dollars. But now armed bandits are after them. When they find a gold Apache statue hidden in a skull, it seems Red Horse is hunting them, too. Then they lose their way, and each step they take in the damp, dark cavern could be their last.

Rodomonte's Revenge

Friends Brett Wilder and Tom Houston are video game whizzes. So when a new virtual reality arcade called Rodomonte's Revenge opens near their home, they make sure they're its first customers. The game is awesome. There are flaming fire rivers to jump, beastly buzz-bugs to fight, and ugly tunnel spiders to escape. If they're good enough they'll face

Rodomonte, an evil giant waiting to do battle within his hidden castle.

But soon after they play the game, strange things start happening to Brett and Tom. The computer is taking over their minds. Now everything that happens in the game is happening in real life. A buzz-bug could gnaw off their ears. Rodomonte could smash them to bits. Brett and Tom have no choice but to play Rodomonte's Revenge again. This time they'll be playing for their lives.

Escape from Fire Mountain

". . . please, anybody . . . fire . . . need help."

That's the urgent cry thirteen-year-old Nikki Roberts hears over the CB radio the weekend she's left alone in her family's hunting lodge. The message also says that the sender is trapped near a bend in the river. Nikki knows it's dangerous, but she has to try to help. She paddles her canoe downriver, coming closer to the thick black smoke of the forest fire with each stroke. When she reaches the bend, Nikki climbs onshore. There, covered with soot and huddled on a rock ledge, sit two small children.

Nikki struggles to get the children to safety. Flames roar around them. Trees splinter to the ground. But as Nikki tries to escape the fire, she doesn't know that two poachers are also hot on her trail. They fear that she and the children have seen too much of their illegal operation—and they'll do anything to keep the kids from making it back to the lodge alive.

The Rock Jockeys

Devil's Wall.

Rick Williams and his friends J.D. and Spud—the Rock Jockeys—are attempting to become the first and youngest climbers to ascend the north face of their area's most treacherous mountain. They're also out to discover if a B-17 bomber rumored to have crashed into the mountain years ago is really there.

As the Rock Jockeys explore Devil's Wall, they stumble upon the plane's battered shell. Inside, they find items that seem to have belonged to the crew, including a diary written by the navigator. Spud later falls into a deep hole and finds something even more frightening: a human skull and bones. To find out where they might have come from, the boys read the navigator's story in the diary. It reveals a gruesome secret that heightens the dangers the mountain might hold for the Rock Jockeys.

Hook 'Em, Snotty!

Bobbie Walker loves working on her grandfather's ranch. She hates the fact that her cousin Alex is coming up from Los Angeles to visit and will probably ruin her summer. Alex can barely ride a horse and doesn't know the first thing about roping. There is no way Alex can survive a ride into the flats to round up wild cattle. But Bobbie is going to have to let her tag along anyway.

Out in the flats the weather turns bad. Even worse, Bobbie knows that she'll have to watch out for the Bledsoe boys, two mischievous brothers who are usually up to no good. When the boys rustle the girls' cattle, Bobbie and Alex team up to teach the Bledsoes a lesson. But with the wild bull Diablo on the loose, the fun and games may soon turn deadly serious.

Danger on Midnight River

Daniel Martin doesn't want to go to Camp Eagle Nest. He wants to spend the summer as he always does: with his uncle Smitty in the Rocky Mountains. Daniel is a slow learner, but most other kids call him retarded. Daniel knows that at camp, things are only going to get worse. His nightmare comes true when he and three bullies must ride the camp van together.

On the trip to camp, Daniel is the butt of the bullies' jokes. He ignores them and concentrates on the roads outside. He thinks they may be lost. As the van crosses a wooden bridge, the planks suddenly give way. The van plunges into the raging river below. Daniel struggles to shore, but the driver and the other boys are nowhere to be found. It's freezing, and night is setting in. Daniel faces a difficult decision. He could save himself . . . or risk everything to try to rescue the others, too.

The Gorgon Slayer

Eleven-year-old Warren Trumbull has a strange job. He works for Prince Charming's Damsel in Distress Rescue Agency, saving people from hideous monsters, evil warlocks, and wicked witches. Then one day Warren gets the most dangerous assignment of all: He must exterminate a Gorgon.

Gorgons are horrible creatures. They have green scales, clawed fingers, and snakes for hair. They also have the power to turn people to stone. Warren doesn't want to be a stone statue for the rest of his life. He'll need all his courage and skill—and his secret plan—to become a true Gorgon slayer.

The Gorgon howls as Warren enters the dark basement to do battle. Warren lowers his eyes, raises his sword and shield, and leaps into action. But will his plan work?

Captive!

Roman Sanchez is trying hard to deal with the death of his dad—a SWAT team member gunned down in the line of duty. But Roman's nightmare is just beginning.

When masked gunmen storm into his classroom, Roman and three other boys are taken hostage. They are thrown into the back of a truck and hauled to a run-down mountain cabin, miles from anywhere. They are bound with rope and given no food. With each passing hour the kidnappers' deadly threats become even more real.

Roman knows time is running out. Now he must

somehow put his dad's death behind him so that he and the others can launch a last desperate fight for freedom.

The Treasure of El Patrón

Tag Jones and his friend Cowboy spend their days diving in the azure water surrounding Bermuda. It's not just for fun—Tag knows that somewhere in the coral reef there's a sunken ship full of treasure. His father died in a diving accident looking for the ship, and Tag won't give up until he finds it.

Then the ship's manifest of the Spanish galleon *El Patrón* turns up, and Tag can barely contain his excitement. *El Patrón* sank in 1614, carrying "unknown cargo." Tag knows that *this* is the ship his father was looking for. And he's not the least bit scared off by the rumors that *El Patrón* is cursed. But when two tourists want Tag to retrieve some mysterious sunken parcels for them, Tag and Cowboy may be in dangerous water, way over their heads!

Skydive!

Jesse Rodriguez has a pretty exciting job for a thirteen-year-old, working at a small flight and skydiving school near Seattle. Buck Sellman, the owner of the school, lets Jesse help out around the airport and is teaching him all about skydiving. Jesse can't wait until he's sixteen and old enough to make his first jump.

Then Robin Waterford walks in with her father

one day to sign up for lessons, and strange things start to happen. Photographs that Robin takes of the airfield mysteriously disappear from her locker. And Robin and Jesse discover that someone at the airfield is involved in an illegal transportation operation. Jesse and Robin soon find themselves in the middle of real danger and are forced to make their first skydives very unexpectedly—using only one parachute!

The Seventh Crystal

Chosen One,

The ancient palace lies in the Valley of Zon. It is imperative that you come immediately. You are my last hope. Look for the secret path. The stars will lead the way. Take care. The eyes of Mogg are everywhere.

As if school bullies weren't enough of a problem, now Chris Masters has a computer game pushing him around! Ever since The Seventh Crystal arrived anonymously in the mail one day, Chris has been obsessed with it—it's the most challenging game he's ever played. But when the game starts to take over, Chris is forced to face a lean, mean, *medieval* bully.

The Creature of Black Water Lake

Thirteen-year-old Ryan Swanner and his mom just moved to the mountain resort of Black Water

Lake. The locals say that beneath the lake's seemingly calm surface, a giant, ancient creature lives. But Ryan's new friend Rita tells him that's just hogwash. She's not afraid to go fishing out on the lake, even though, oddly, the lake seems to be nearly empty of fish. One day Ryan sees a small animal fall from a tree into the lake—and never surface again. Something *is* in the lake. And it's alive. . . .

Time Benders

Superbrain Zack Griffin and hoops fanatic Jeff Brown wouldn't normally hang together. But when both boys win trips to a famous science laboratory, they find out they have one thing in common: a serious case of curiosity. And when they sneak into the lab to check out the time-bending machine again, they end up in Egypt—in 1334 B.C.!

Grizzly

Justin swallowed and pointed the light at the soft dirt. The tracks were plain: two large pads with five long scissorlike claws on each.

A grizzly.

A grizzly bear is terrorizing the sheep ranch that belongs to Justin McCallister's aunt and uncle. First the grizzly takes a swipe at the ranch's guard dog, Old Molly. Then he kills several sheep and injures Justin's collie, Radar. When the grizzly kills Blue,

Justin's pet lamb, Justin decides to take matters into his own hands. He sets out to track down the bear himself. But what will Justin do when he comes face to face with the grizzly?

Thunder Valley

Jeremy Parsons and his twin Brother, Jason, have been left on their own to run the family business, Thunder Valley Ski Lodge. But ever since Grandpa broke his hip and Grandma went with him to the hospital, strange things have been happening. Things even stranger than the fire in the snowmobile garage. Jason and Jeremy had better find out who's responsible, because Thunder Valley is going downhill fast.

Curse of the Ruins

"A few hundred yards ahead there is a long wooden bridge that the donkeys will be afraid to cross. But do not worry. After you cross the bridge, the ruins will not be far away."

Cousins Katie, Sam, and Shala quickly see why the donkeys are so afraid to cross the bridge—it's old and rickety and spans a deep, rocky canyon. But they have to get across it. They have to find Katie and Sam's dad, an anthropologist who's studying the ancient cliff dwellers at El Debajo. Dr. Crockett was supposed to meet the cousins at the airport in

San Marcos, New Mexico, but he never showed up. They don't know whether he has enemies who might have kidnapped him or whether there really is a curse on the ruins of El Debajo. But they're about to find out.